The Festival

STEPHANIE

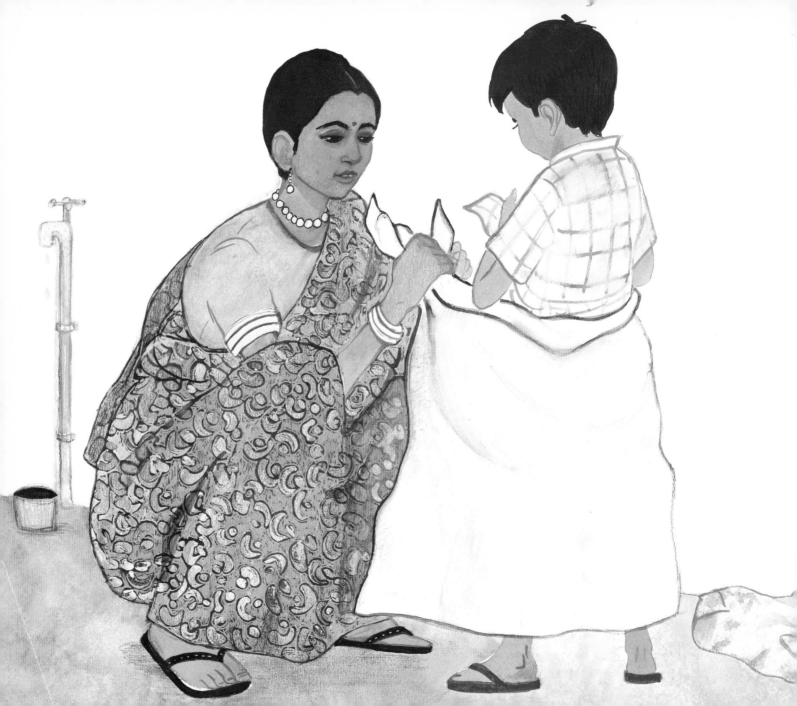

The Festival

Story by Peter Bonnici
Pictures by Lisa Kopper

Carolrhoda Books, Inc./Minneapolis

LIBRARY OF CONGRESS CATALOGING IN PUBLICATION DATA

Bonnici, Peter.
The festival.

Summary: A young Indian boy experiences for the first
time the rituals of manhood at the village festival.
1. Children's stories, American. [1. India — Fiction]
I. Kopper, Lisa, ill. II. Title.
PZ7.B64254Fe 1985 [E] 84-15597
ISBN 0-87614-229-3 (lib. bdg.)

2C1691

This edition first published 1985 by Carolrhoda Books, Inc.
Original edition published 1984
by Bell & Hyman Limited, London, England.
Text copyright © 1984 by Peter Bonnici.
Illustrations copyright © 1984 by Lisa Kopper.
All rights reserved.

Manufactured in the United States of America

1 2 3 4 5 6 7 8 9 10 94 93 92 91 90 89 88 87 86 85

Arjuna found visits to his grandmother's village dull.
He spent all his time staring at lizards or picking berries.
Then one day his grandmother announced,
"The time has come to start preparations
for our special festival." Her words were like the wind,
creating movement everywhere.

Arjuna's mother got out the colored powders, which she poured into the most beautiful designs on the front step. "Is it the festival of holi when I go around splashing color on everyone?" Arjuna asked.

His mother said, "No."

Aunt Seeta was busy cooking sweets over a tiny
charcoal stove that cracked and sparked, shooting embers
across the yard. Arjuna's eyes lit up. "Aha," he said.
"Then it must be divali with rockets and sparklers
and bangers that are as loud as bombs."
His aunt smiled. "No bombs," she said.

"Grandma, you tell me," Arjuna begged as he watched
his grandmother hang garlands of mango leaves over
the doors and windows. "Oh nuisance child," she said.
"It is the festival of our village temple. Now let us get on."
"Okay," said Arjuna quietly. "I only thought it was something
really special." He spent the rest of the day picking berries,
his face just like the mango leaves—all long and twisting.

That evening his mother came up to him
as he was washing the purple berry stains
from his fingers.
"Stop acting like an old crow," she said
and pulled out a brown paper package
from behind her back.
It was a lungi—Arjuna's first.
His mother tied it around his waist.
"There," she said.
"You look just like one of the men
from our village."

Uncle Raju clapped him on the shoulder. "Now you must take a bath in the pond like the rest of the men," he said.

Much to Arjuna's horror, the whole event
was spied upon by a group of giggling girls
and shared by two sleepy water buffalo.

That night the temple courtyard had been transformed
into a fairyland of light and color.
Arjuna too had been transformed.
For the first time he was to sit among the men,
his hair all shiny with coconut oil
and around his waist the new lungi.

The festivities began.
Arjuna danced and chanted
with the men,
clashing his cymbals,
turning round and round
the temple shrine.
The women sat to one side
and made a high
wobbling sound
with their tongues.

And then—right in the middle of the
dancing—something awful happened.
Arjuna felt his lungi go slack and
slip off. The shock! The shame!
He wished the world
would come to an end.

But, swift as a cobra, there was Uncle Raju,
his face all covered with sweat.
He swept Arjuna onto his shoulder.
"This is no time for tears," he said. "It's time for eating."
He carried Arjuna out of the temple square,
through a narrow alleyway and into a tiny yard
where the old men had gathered to tell stories.

Together they sat on a rope cot
and ate chapatis cooked over glowing coals
and listened to the stories of the old men
till the full moon shone as yellow
and as bright as the sun.

As they made their sleepy way home that night
beneath the enormous black trees
that sparkled with fireflies,
Arjuna's mind filled over and over again
with the words of the village headman,
"Best among the dancers tonight
was the newest son of our village—Arjuna."

A Note from Arjuna

My home in India is the city. It's huge and bustling and very exciting. But most people in India live in villages like my grandmother's. Life in the village is very slow. People work hard. The sun in the fields is hot—like the devil's breath. So when it is time for a celebration, everyone enters into the fun of things.

The festival of *holi* is to celebrate the colors of spring. All over India— in the cities and in the villages—we enjoy *holi.* You must make sure to wear your old clothes, though, because without any warning someone might splash colored water or powder over you. We all do it.

All round the world people have a special day for fireworks, and so too in India. *Divali* is our festival of light. The black sky bursts alive with rockets and the quiet evening is shattered with the cracking and booming of firecrackers. In India people like firecrackers best—especially the large square ones which we call box bombs because of the enormous booms they make.

And India wouldn't be India without festivals to the gods. Every state, every village, every home has its own favorite god. During these festivals there is plenty of music and dancing and eating. Best of all the things to eat are the sweets.

My Aunt Seeta is an expert sweetmaker. She makes *gulab jamuns* best— milk and flour, ground almonds and sugar rolled into tiny balls, fried in her large pan, and then soaked in syrup with a little rose water in it. My mouth is watering just to think about them. And there are *chapatis* too. These are flat like pancakes but made with flour and water only. I eat mine with plenty of sugar.

All this talk about food has built up my appetite. I'm off to scrounge a stick of sugarcane from the man in the courtyard downstairs.